"His poems are easy to read, which is a pleasure in itself . . . you're startled by what's being set down, or by a single twist either in content or in image, or by the honesty with which the poet is expressing himself. . . .

—*Poetry*

"They are pretty special poems, for if Brautigan never writes another one, he will have left a great amount of poetry in our literature."
—*The Seattle Times*

RICHARD BRAUTIGAN is also the author of *Trout Fishing in America*, *Revenge of the Lawn*, *Rommel Drives on Deep into Egypt*, *The Abortion: An Historical Romance 1966* and *In Watermelon Sugar*.

Writing 20

RICHARD BRAUTIGAN

The Pill
Versus
The Springhill Mine
Disaster

Published by
Dell Publishing Co., Inc.
1 Dag Hammarskjold Plaza
New York, New York 10017

ISBN: 0-440-36956-8

This book was first published by
Four Seasons Foundation in its
Writing series edited by Donald Allen

Cover photograph by Edmund Shea

Manufactured in the United States of America
First Laurel printing—August 1973
Second Laurel printing—March 1974
Third Laurel printing—April 1975
Fourth Laurel printing—May 1976
Fifth Laurel printing—April 1977

This book is for
Miss Marcia Pacaud of Montreal, Canada.

Contents

The Pill Versus the Springhill Mine Disaster

All Watched Over by Machines of Loving Grace

I like to think (and
the sooner the better!)
of a cybernetic meadow
where mammals and computers
live together in mutually
programming harmony
like pure water
touching clear sky.

I like to think
   (right now, please!)
of a cybernetic forest
filled with pines and electronics
where deer stroll peacefully
past computers
as if they were flowers
with spinning blossoms.

I like to think
   (it has to be!)
of a cybernetic ecology
where we are free of our labors
and joined back to nature,
returned to our mammal
brothers and sisters,
and all watched over
by machines of loving grace.

Horse Child Breakfast

Horse child breakfast,
what are you doing to me?
with your long blonde legs?
with your long blonde face?
with your long blonde hair?
with your perfect blonde ass?

I swear I'll never be the
    same again!

Horse child breakfast,
what you're doing to me,
I want done forever.

General Custer Versus the Titanic

For the soldiers of the Seventh Cavalry who were killed at the Little Bighorn River and the passengers who were lost on the maiden voyage of the Titanic.
God bless their souls.

Yes! it's true all my visions
have come home to roost at last.
They are all true now and stand
around me like a bouquet of
lost ships and doomed generals.
I gently put them away in a
beautiful and disappearing vase.

The Beautiful Poem

I go to bed in Los Angeles thinking
   about you.

Pissing a few moments ago
I looked down at my penis
   affectionately.

Knowing it has been inside
you twice today makes me
   feel beautiful.

          3 A.M.
          January 15, 1967

Private Eye Lettuce

Three crates of Private Eye Lettuce,
the name and drawing of a detective
with magnifying glass on the sides
of the crates of lettuce,
form a great cross in man's imagination
and his desire to name
the objects of this world.
I think I'll call this place Golgotha
and have some salad for dinner.

A Boat

O beautiful
was the werewolf
in his evil forest.
We took him
to the carnival
and he started
    crying
when he saw
the Ferris wheel.
Electric
green and red tears
flowed down
his furry cheeks.
He looked
like a boat
out on the dark
water.

The Shenevertakesherwatchoff Poem

For Marcia

Because you always have a clock
strapped to your body, it's natural
that I should think of you as the
    correct time:
with your long blonde hair at 8:03,
and your pulse-lightning breasts at
11:17, and your rose-meow smile at 5:30,
    I know I'm right.

Karma Repair Kit: Items 1–4

1. Get enough food to eat,
   and eat it.

2. Find a place to sleep where it is quiet,
   and sleep there.

3. Reduce intellectual and emotional noise
   until you arrive at the silence of yourself,
   and listen to it.

4.

Oranges

Oh, how perfect death
computes an orange wind
that glows from your footsteps,

and you stop to die in
an orchard where the harvest
fills the stars.

San Francisco

This poem was found written on a paper bag by Richard Brautigan in a laundromat in San Francisco. The author is unknown.

By accident, you put
Your money in my
Machine (#4)
By accident, I put
My money in another
Machine (#6)
On purpose, I put
Your clothes in the
Empty machine full
Of water and no
Clothes

It was lonely.

Xerox Candy Bar

Ah,
you're just a copy
of all the candy bars
I've ever eaten.

Discovery

The petals of the vagina unfold
like Christopher Columbus
taking off his shoes.

Is there anything more beautiful
than the bow of a ship
touching a new world?

Widow's Lament

It's not quite cold enough
to go borrow some firewood
from the neighbors.

The Pomegranate Circus

I am desolate in dimension
circling the sky
              like a rainy bird,

wet from toe to crown
wet from bill to wing.

I feel like a drowned king
at the pomegranate circus.

I vowed last year
that I wouldn't go again
but here I sit in my usual seat,
   dripping and clapping

as the pomegranates go by
in their metallic costumes.

December 25, 1966

The Winos on Potrero Hill

Alas, they get
their bottles
from a small
neighborhood store.
The old Russian
sells them port
and passes no moral
judgment. They go
and sit under
the green bushes
that grow along
the wooden stairs.
They could almost
be exotic flowers,
they drink so
quietly.

The First Winter Snow

Oh, pretty girl, you have trapped
yourself in the wrong body. Twenty
extra pounds hang like a lumpy
tapestry on your perfect mammal nature.

Three months ago you were like a
deer staring at the first winter snow.

Now Aphrodite thumbs her nose at you
and tells stories behind your back.

Death Is a Beautiful Car Parked Only

For Emmett

Death is a beautiful car parked only
to be stolen on a street lined with trees
whose branches are like the intestines
   of an emerald.

You hotwire death, get in, and drive away
like a flag made from a thousand burning
   funeral parlors.

You have stolen death because you're bored.
There's nothing good playing at the movies
   in San Francisco.

You joyride around for a while listening
to the radio, and then abandon death, walk
away, and leave death for the police
   to find.

Surprise

I lift the toilet seat
    as if it were the nest of a bird
and I see cat tracks
    all around the edge of the bowl.

Your Departure Versus the Hindenburg

Every time we say good-bye
I see it as an extension of
   the Hindenburg:
that great 1937 airship exploding
in medieval flames like a burning castle
   above New Jersey.
When you leave the house, the
shadow of the Hindenburg enters
   to take your place.

Education

There is a woman
on the Klamath River
who has five
hundred children
in the basement,
stuffed like
hornets into
a mud nest.
Great Sparrow
is their father.
Once a day
he pulls a
red wagon between
them and
that's all
they know.

Love Poem

It's so nice
to wake up in the morning
  all alone
and not have to tell somebody
  you love them
when you don't love them
  any more.

The Fever Monument

I walked across the park to the fever monument.
It was in the center of a glass square surrounded
by red flowers and fountains. The monument
was in the shape of a sea horse and the plaque read
We got hot and died.

At the California Institute of Technology

I don't care how God-damn smart
these guys are: I'm bored.

It's been raining like hell all day long
and there's nothing to do.

> *Written January 24, 1967*
> *while poet-in-residence at*
> *the California Institute of*
> *Technology.*

A Lady

Her face grips at her mouth
like a leaf to a tree
or a tire to a highway
or a spoon to a bowl of soup.

She just can't let go
    with a smile,
    the poor dear.

No matter what happens
her face is always a maple tree
    Highway 101
    tomato.

"Star-Spangled" Nails

You've got
some "Star-Spangled"
   nails
in your coffin, kid.
That's what
they've done for you,
   son.

The Pumpkin Tide

I saw thousands of pumpkins last night
come floating in on the tide,
bumping up against the rocks and
rolling up on the beaches;
it must be Halloween in the sea.

Adrenalin Mother

Adrenalin Mother,
with your dress of comets
and shoes of swift bird wings
and shadow of jumping fish,
thank you for touching,
understanding and loving my life.
Without you, I am dead.

The Wheel

The wheel: it's a thing like pears
rotting under a tree in August.
O golden wilderness!
The bees travel in covered wagons
and the Indians hide in the heat.

Map Shower

For Marcia

I want your hair
to cover me with maps
of new places,

so everywhere I go
will be as beautiful
as your hair.

A Postcard from Chinatown

The Chinese smoke opium
in their bathrooms.
They all get in the bathroom
and lock the door.
The old people sit in the tub
and the children sit
on the floor.

The Double-Bed Dream Gallows

Driving through
hot brushy country
in the late autumn,
I saw a hawk
crucified on a
barbed-wire fence.

I guess as a kind
of advertisement
to other hawks,
saying from the pages
of a leading women's
    magazine,

"She's beautiful,
but burn all the maps
to your body.
I'm not here
of my own choosing."

December 30

At 1:03 in the morning a fart
smells like a marriage between
an avocado and a fish head.

I have to get out of bed
to write this down without
    my glasses on.

The Sawmill

I am the sawmill
abandoned even by the ghost.
in the middle of a pasture.
  Opera!
    Opera!
The horses won't go near
my God-damn thing.
They stay over by the creek.

The Way She Looks at It

Every time I see him, I think:
Gee, am I glad he's not
    my old man.

Yes, the Fish Music

A trout-colored wind blows
through my eyes, through my fingers,
and I remember how the trout
used to hide from the dinosaurs
when they came to drink at the river.
The trout hid in subways, castles
and automobiles. They waited patiently
for the dinosaurs to go away.

The Chinese Checker Players

When I was six years old
I played Chinese checkers
   with a woman
who was ninety-three years old.
She lived by herself
in an apartment down the hall
   from ours.
We played Chinese checkers
every Monday and Thursday nights.
While we played she usually talked
about her husband
who had been dead for seventy years,
and we drank tea and ate cookies
   and cheated.

I've Never Had It Done so Gently Before

For M

The sweet juices of your mouth
are like castles bathed in honey.
I've never had it done so gently before.
You have put a circle of castles
around my penis and you swirl them
like sunlight on the wings of birds.

Our Beautiful West Coast Thing

We are a coast people
There is nothing but ocean out beyond us.
—Jack Spicer

I sit here dreaming
long thoughts of California
at the end of a November day
below a cloudy twilight
    near the Pacific

listening to The Mamas and The Papas
    THEY'RE GREAT

singing a song about breaking
somebody's heart and digging it!

I think I'll get up
and dance around the room.

    Here I go!

Man

With his hat on
he's about five inches taller
than a taxicab.

The Silver Stairs of Ketchikan

2 A.M. is the best time
to climb the silver stairs
of Ketchikan and go up into the trees
and the dark prowling deer.

When my wife gets out of bed
to feed the baby at 2 A.M., she turns
on all the lights in Ketchikan
and people start banging on the doors
and swearing at one another.

That's the best time
to climb the silver stairs
of Ketchikan and go up into the trees
and the dark prowling deer.

Hollywood

January 26, 1967
at 3:15 in the afternoon

Sitting here in Los Angeles
parked on a rundown residential
   back street,
staring up at the word
   HOLLYWOOD
written on some lonely mountains,
I'm listening very carefully
to rock and roll radio
   (Lovin' Spoonful)
   (Jefferson Airplane)
while people are slowly
putting out their garbage cans.

Your Necklace Is Leaking

For Marcia

Your necklace is leaking
and blue light drips
from your beads to cover
your beautiful breasts
with a clear African dawn.

Haiku Ambulance

A piece of green pepper
    fell
off the wooden salad bowl:
    so what?

It's Going Down

Magic is the color of the thing you wear
with a dragon for a button
and a lion for a lamp
with a carrot for a collar
and a salmon for a zipper.

Hey! You're turning me on: baby.
That's the way it's going down.

WOW!

Alas, Measured Perfectly

Saturday, August 25, 1888. 5:20 P.M.
is the name of a photograph of two
old women in a front yard, beside
a white house. One of the women is
sitting in a chair with a dog in her
lap. The other woman is looking at
some flowers. Perhaps the women are
happy, but then it is Saturday, August
25, 1888. 5:21 P.M., and all over.

Hey, Bacon!

The moon like:
mischievous bacon
crisps its desire

(while)

I harbor myself
toward two eggs
over easy.

The Rape of Ophelia

Her clothes spread wide and mermaid-like awhile
they bore her up: which time she chanted snatches
of old tunes, and sweet Ophelia floated down the river
past black stones until she came to an evil fisherman
who was dressed in clothes that had no childhood,
and beautiful Ophelia floated like an April church
into his shadow, and he, the evil fisherman of our
dreams, waded out into the river and captured the
poor mad girl, and taking her into the deep grass, he
killed her with the shock of his body, and he placed
her back into the river, and Laertes said, Alas, then
she is drown'd! Too much of water has thou,
poor Ophelia.

A CandleLion Poem

For Michael

Turn a candle inside out
and you've got the smallest
portion of a lion standing
there at the edge of the
  shadows.

I Feel Horrible. She Doesn't

I feel horrible. She doesn't
love me and I wander around
the house like a sewing machine
that's just finished sewing
a turd to a garbage can lid.

Cyclops

A glass of lemonade
travels across this world
like the eye of the cyclops.

If a child doesn't drink
the lemonade,
   Ulysses will.

Flowers for Those You Love

Butcher, baker, candlestick maker,
anybody can get VD,
including those you love.

Please see a doctor
if you think you've got it.

You'll feel better afterwards
and so will those you love.

THE GALILEE HITCH-HIKER

The Galilee Hitch-Hiker
Part 1

Baudelaire was
driving a Model A
across Galilee.
He picked up a
hitch-hiker named
Jesus who had
been standing among
a school of fish,
feeding them
pieces of bread.
"Where are you
going?" asked
Jesus, getting
into the front
seat.
"Anywhere, anywhere
out of this world!"
shouted
Baudelaire.
"I'll go with you
as far as
Golgotha,"
said Jesus.
"I have a
concession
at the carnival
there, and I
must not be
late."

The American Hotel
Part 2

Baudelaire was sitting
in a doorway with a wino
on San Francisco's skidrow.
The wino was a million
years old and could remember
    dinosaurs.
Baudelaire and the wino
were drinking Petri Muscatel.
"One must always be drunk,"
    said Baudelaire.
"I live in the American Hotel,"
said the wino. "And I can
    remember dinosaurs."
"Be you drunken ceaselessly,"
    said Baudelaire.

1939
   Part 3

Baudelaire used to come
to our house and watch
me grind coffee.
That was in 1939
and we lived in the slums
of Tacoma.
My mother would put
the coffee beans in the grinder.
I was a child
and would turn the handle,
pretending that it was
   a hurdy-gurdy,
and Baudelaire would pretend
that he was a monkey,
hopping up and down
and holding out
a tin cup.

The Flowerburgers
Part 4

Baudelaire opened
up a hamburger stand
in San Francisco,
but he put flowers
between the buns.
People would come in
and say, "Give me a
hamburger with plenty
of onions on it."
Baudelaire would give
them a flowerburger
instead and the people
would say, "What kind
of a hamburger stand
is this?"

The Hour of Eternity
Part 5

"The Chinese
read the time
in the eyes
of cats,"
said Baudelaire
and went into
a jewelry store
on Market Street.
He came out
a few moments
later carrying
a twenty-one
jewel Siamese
cat that he
wore on the
end of a
golden chain.

Salvador Dali
Part 6

"Are you
or aren't you
going to eat
your soup,
you bloody old
cloud merchant?"
Jeanne Duval
shouted,
hitting Baudelaire
on the back
as he sat
daydreaming
out the window.
Baudelaire was
startled.
Then he laughed
like hell,
waving his spoon
in the air
like a wand
changing the room
into a painting
by Salvador
Dali, changing
the room
into a painting
by Van Gogh.

A Baseball Game
Part 7

Baudelaire went
to a baseball game
and bought a hot dog
and lit up a pipe
of opium.
The New York Yankees
were playing
the Detroit Tigers.
In the fourth inning
an angel committed
suicide by jumping
off a low cloud.
The angel landed
on second base,
causing the
whole infield
to crack like
a huge mirror.
The game was
called on
account of
fear.

Insane Asylum
Part 8

Baudelaire went
to the insane asylum
disguised as a
psychiatrist.
He stayed there
for two months
and when he left,
the insane asylum
loved him so much
that it followed
him all over
California,
and Baudelaire
laughed when the
insane asylum
rubbed itself
up against his
leg like a
strange cat.

My Insect Funeral
Part 9

When I was a child
I had a graveyard
where I buried insects
and dead birds under
a rose tree.
I would bury the insects
in tin foil and match boxes.
I would bury the birds
in pieces of red cloth.
It was all very sad
and I would cry
as I scooped the dirt
into their small graves
with a spoon.
Baudelaire would come
and join in
my insect funerals,
saying little prayers
the size of
dead birds.

San Francisco
February 1958

It's Raining in Love

I don't know what it is,
but I distrust myself
when I start to like a girl
   a lot.

It makes me nervous.
I don't say the right things
or perhaps I start
   to examine,
                  evaluate,
                           compute
   what I am saying.

If I say, "Do you think it's going to rain?"
and she says, "I don't know,"
I start thinking: Does she really like me?

In other words
I get a little creepy.

A friend of mine once said,
"It's twenty times better to be friends
   with someone
than it is to be in love with them."

I think he's right and besides,
it's raining somewhere, programming flowers
and keeping snails happy.
   That's all taken care of.

         BUT
if a girl likes me a lot
and starts getting real nervous
and suddenly begins asking me funny questions

and looks sad if I give the wrong answers
and she says things like,
"Do you think it's going to rain?"
and I say, "It beats me,"
and she says, "Oh,"
and looks a little sad
at the clear blue California sky,
I think: Thank God, it's you, baby, this time
   instead of me.

Poker Star

It's a star that looks
like a poker game above
the mountains of eastern
    Oregon.
There are three men playing.
They are all sheepherders.
One of them has two pair,
the others have nothing.

To England

There are no postage stamps that send letters
back to England three centuries ago,
no postage stamps that make letters
travel back until the grave hasn't been dug yet,
and John Donne stands looking out the window,
it is just beginning to rain this April morning,
and the birds are falling into the trees
like chess pieces into an unplayed game,
and John Donne sees the postman
coming up the street,
the postman walks very carefully
because his cane is made
of glass.

I Lie Here in a Strange Girl's Apartment

For Marcia

I lie here in a strange girl's apartment.
She has poison oak, a bad sunburn
   and is unhappy.
She moves about the place
like distant gestures of solemn glass.

She opens and closes things.
She turns the water on,
and she turns the water off.

All the sounds she makes are faraway.
They could be in a different city.
It is dusk and people are staring
out the windows of that city.
Their eyes are filled with the sounds
   of what she is doing.

Hey! This Is What It's All About

For Jeff Sheppard

No publication
No money
No star
No fuck

   A friend came over to the house
a few days ago and read one of my poems.
He came back today and asked to read the
same poem over again. After he finished
reading it, he said, "It makes me want
   to write poetry."

My Nose Is Growing Old

Yup.
A long lazy September look
in the mirror
says it's true:

I'm 31
and my nose is growing
   old.

It starts about 1/2
   an inch
below the bridge
and strolls geriatrically
   down
for another inch or so:
   stopping.

Fortunately, the rest
of the nose is comparatively
   young.

I wonder if girls
will want me with an
   old nose.

I can hear them now
the heartless bitches!

"He's cute
            but his nose
is old."

Crab Cigar

I was watching a lot of crabs
eating in the tide pools
of the Pacific a few days ago.

When I say a lot: I mean
hundred of crabs. They eat
  like cigars.

The Sidney Greenstreet Blues

I think something beautiful
and amusing is gained
by remembering Sidney Greenstreet,
but it is a fragile thing.

The hand picks up a glass.
The eye looks at the glass
and then hand, glass and eye
 fall away.

Comets

There are comets
that flash through
our mouths wearing
the grace
of oceans and galaxies.

  God knows,
  we try to do the best
  we can.

There are comets
connected to chemicals
that telescope
down our tongues
to burn out against
the air.

  I know
  we do.

There are comets
that laugh at us
from behind our teeth
wearing the clothes
of fish and birds.

  We try.

I Live in the Twentieth Century

For Marcia

I live in the Twentieth Century
and you lie here beside me. You
were unhappy when you fell asleep.
There was nothing I could do about
it. I felt helpless. Your face
is so beautiful that I cannot stop
to describe it, and there's nothing
I can do to make you happy while
    you sleep.

The Castle of the Cormorants

Hamlet with
a cormorant
under his arm
married Ophelia.
She was still
wet from drowning.
She looked like
a white flower
that had been
left in the
rain too long.
I love you,
said Ophelia,
and I love
that dark
bird you
hold in
your arms.

Big Sur
February 1958

Lovers

I changed her bedroom:
raised the ceiling four feet,
removed all of her things
(and the clutter of her life)
painted the walls white,
placed a fantastic calm
  in the room,
a silence that almost had a scent,
put her in a low brass bed
with white satin covers,
and I stood there in the doorway
watching her sleep, curled up,
with her face turned away
  from me.

Sonnet

The sea is like .
an old nature poet
who died of a
heart attack in a
public latrine.
His ghost still
haunts the urinals.
At night he can
be heard walking
around barefooted
in the dark.
Somebody stole
his shoes.

Indirect Popcorn

What a good time fancy!
like a leisure white interior
with long yellow curtains.
I'll take it to sleep with me tonight
and hope that my dreams are built
toward beautiful blonde women eating
    indirect popcorn.

Star Hole

I sit here
on the perfect end
of a star,

watching light
pour itself toward
    me.

The light pours
itself through
a small hole
in the sky.

I'm not very happy,
but I can see
how things are
  faraway.

Albion Breakfast

For Susan

Last night (here) a long pretty girl
asked me to write a poem about Albion,
so she could put it in a black folder
that has albion printed nicely
    in white on the cover.

I said yes. She's at the store now
getting something for breakfast.
I'll surprise her with this poem
    when she gets back.

Let's Voyage into the New American House

There are doors
that want to be free
from their hinges to
fly with perfect clouds.

There are windows
that want to be
released from their
frames to run with
the deer through
back country meadows.

There are walls
that want to prowl
with the mountains
through the early
morning dusk.

There are floors
that want to digest
their furniture into
flowers and trees.

There are roofs
that want to travel
gracefully with
the stars through
circles of darkness.

November 3

I'm sitting in a cafe,
drinking a Coke.

A fly is sleeping
on a paper napkin.

I have to wake him up,
so I can wipe my glasses.

There's a pretty girl
I want to look at.

The Postman

The smell
          of vegetables
                    on a cold day
performs faithfully an act of reality
like a knight in search of the holy grail
or a postman on a rural route looking
for a farm that isn't there.
  Carrots, peppers and berries.
  Nerval, Baudelaire and Rimbaud.

A Mid-February Sky Dance

Dance toward me, please, as
if you were a star
with light-years piled
on top of your hair,
   smiling,

and I will dance toward you
as if I were darkness
with bats piled like a hat
   on top of my head.

The Quail

There are three quail in a cage next door,
and they are the sweet delight of our mornings,
calling to us like small frosted cakes:
   bobwhitebobwhitebobwhite,
but at night they drive our God-damn cat Jake crazy.
They run around that cage like pinballs
as he stands out there,
smelling their asses through the wire.

1942

Piano tree, play
in the dark concert halls
of my uncle,
twenty-six years old, dead
and homeward bound
on a ship from Sitka,
his coffin travels
like the fingers
of Beethoven
over a glass
of wine.

Piano tree, play
in the dark concert halls
of my uncle,
a legend of my childhood, dead,
they send him back
to Tacoma.
At night his coffin
travels like the birds
that fly beneath the sea,
never touching the sky.

Piano tree, play
in the dark concert halls
of my uncle,
take his heart
for a lover
and take his death
for a bed,
and send him homeward bound
on a ship from Sitka
to bury him
where I was born.

Milk for the Duck

ZAP!
unlaid / 20 days

my sexual image
isn't worth a shit.

If I were dead
I couldn't attract
a female fly.

The Return of the Rivers

All the rivers run into the sea;
yet the sea is not full;
unto the place from whence the rivers come,
thither they return again.

It is raining today
in the mountains.

It is a warm green rain
with love
in its pockets
for spring is here,
and does not dream
of death.

Birds happen music
like clocks ticking heavens
in a land
where children love spiders,
and let them sleep
in their hair.

A slow rain sizzles
on the river
like a pan
full of frying flowers,
and with each drop
of rain
the ocean
begins again.

A Good-Talking Candle

I had a good-talking candle
last night in my bedroom.

I was very tired but I wanted
somebody to be with me,
   so I lit a candle

and listened to its comfortable
voice of light until I was asleep.

The Horse That Had a Flat Tire

Once upon a valley
there came down
from some goldenblue mountains
a handsome young prince
who was riding
a dawncolored horse
named Lordsburg.

I love you
You're my breathing castle
Gentle so gentle
We'll live forever

In the valley
there was a beautiful maiden
whom the prince
drifted into love with
like a New Mexico made from
apple thunder and long
glass beds.

I love you
You're my breathing castle
Gentle so gentle
We'll live forever

The prince enchanted
the maiden
and they rode off
on the dawncolored horse
named Lordsburg
toward the goldenblue mountains.

I love you
You're my breathing castle
Gentle so gentle
We'll live forever

They would have lived
happily ever after
if the horse hadn't had
a flat tire
in front of a dragon's
house.

Kafka's Hat

With the rain falling
surgically against the roof,
I ate a dish of ice cream
that looked like Kafka's hat.

It was a dish of ice cream
tasting like an operating table
with the patient staring
up at the ceiling.

Nine Things

It's night

and a numbered beauty
lapses at the wind,

chortles with the
branches of a tree,

   giggles,

plays shadow dance
with a dead kite,

cajoles affection
from falling leaves,

and knows four
other things.

One is the color
of your hair.

Linear Farewell, Nonlinear Farewell

When he went out the door,
he said he wasn't coming back,
but he came back, the son-
ofabitch, and now I'm pregnant,
and he won't get off his ass.

Mating Saliva

A girl in a green mini-
skirt, not very pretty, walks
  down the street.

A businessman stops, turns
to stare at her ass
that looks like a moldy
  refrigerator.

There are now 200,000,000 people
  in America.

Sit Comma and Creeley Comma

It's spring and the nun
like a black frog
builds her tarpaper shack
beside the lake.
How beautiful she is
(and looks) surrounded
by her rolls of tarpaper.
They know her name
and they speak her name.

Automatic Anthole

Driven by hunger, I had another
forced bachelor dinner tonight.
I had a lot of trouble making
up my mind whether to eat Chinese
food or have a hamburger. God,
I hate eating dinner alone. It's
    like being dead.

The Symbol

When I was hitch-hiking down to Big Sur,
Moby Dick stopped and picked me up. He was driving
a truckload of sea gulls to San Luis Obispo.

"Do you like being a truckdriver better than you
do a whale?" I asked.

"Yeah," Moby Dick said. "Hoffa is a lot better
to us whales than Captain Ahab ever was.

The old fart."

I Cannot Answer You Tonight in Small Portions

I cannot answer you tonight in small portions.
Torn apart by stormy love's gate, I float
like a phantom facedown in a well where
the cold dark water reflects vague half-built
                    stars
and trades all our affection, touching, sleeping
together for tribunal distance standing like
a drowned train just beyond a pile of Eskimo
                skeletons.

Your Catfish Friend

If I were to live my life
in catfish forms
in scaffolds of skin and whiskers
at the bottom of a pond
and you were to come by
   one evening
when the moon was shining
down into my dark home
and stand there at the edge
   of my affection
and think, "It's beautiful
here by this pond. I wish
   somebody loved me,"
I'd love you and be your catfish
friend and drive such lonely
thoughts from your mind
and suddenly you would be
   at peace,
and ask yourself, "I wonder
if there are any catfish
in this pond? It seems like
a perfect place for them."

November 24

She's mending the rain with her hair.
She's turning the darkness on.
  Glue / switch!
That's all I have to report.

Horse Race

July 19, a dog has been run over by an airplane,
an act that brings into this world the energy
that transforms vultures into beautiful black
   race horses.

Yes, the horses are waiting at the starting gate.
Now the sound of the gun and this fantastic race
begins. The horses are circling the track.

The Pill Versus the Springhill Mine Disaster

When you take your pill
it's like a mine disaster.
I think of all the people
   lost inside of you.

After Halloween Slump

My magic is down.
My spells mope around
the house like sick old dogs
with bloodshot eyes
watering cold wet noses.

My charms are in a pile
in the corner like the
dirty shirts of a summer fatman.

One of my potions died
last night in the pot.
It looks like a cracked
Egyptian tablecloth.

Gee, You're so Beautiful
That It's Starting to Rain

Oh, Marcia,
I want your long blonde beauty
to be taught in high school,
so kids will learn that God
lives like music in the skin
and sounds like a sunshine harpsichord.
I want high school report cards
    to look like this:

Playing with Gentle Glass Things
    A

Computer Magic
    A

Writing Letters to Those You Love
    A

Finding out about Fish
    A

Marcia's Long Blonde Beauty
    A+!

The Nature Poem

The moon
is Hamlet
on a motorcycle
coming down
a dark road.
He is wearing
a black leather
jacket and
boots.
I have
nowhere
to go.
I will ride
all night.

The Day They Busted the Grateful Dead

The day they busted the Grateful Dead
rain stormed against San Francisco
like hot swampy scissors cutting Justice
into the evil clothes that alligators wear.

The day they busted the Grateful Dead
was like a flight of winged alligators
carefully measuring marble with black
   rubber telescopes.

The day they busted the Grateful Dead
turned like the wet breath of alligators
blowing up balloons the size of the
   Hall of Justice.

The Harbor

Torn apart by the storms of love
and put back together by the calms
   of love,

I lie here in a harbor
that does not know
where your body ends
and my body begins.

Fish swim between our ribs
and sea gulls cry like mirrors
   to our blood.

The Garlic Meat Lady from

We're cooking dinner tonight.
I'm making a kind of Stonehenge
   stroganoff.
Marcia is helping me. You
already know the legend
   of her beauty.
I've asked her to rub garlic
on the meat. She takes
each piece of meat like a lover
and rubs it gently with garlic.
I've never seen anything like this
   before. Every orifice
of the meat is explored, caressed
   relentlessly with garlic.
There is a passion here that would
drive a deaf saint to learn
the violin and play Beethoven at
   Stonehenge.

In a Cafe

I watched a man in a cafe fold a slice of bread
as if he were folding a birth certificate or looking
at the photograph of a dead lover.

Boo, Forever

Spinning like a ghost
on the bottom of a
    top,
I'm haunted by all
the space that I
will live without
    you.